PUG

PUG

by Ethan Long

Holiday House / New York

Pug sees Peg.

Pug sees Mom.

Pug sees Dad.

yap Yap Yap
Yap
Yap
Yap Yap

Pug sees Tad.

Tad sees Pug.

Pug wants to go.

No, Pug, no.

Go, Pug, go.

No Peg.

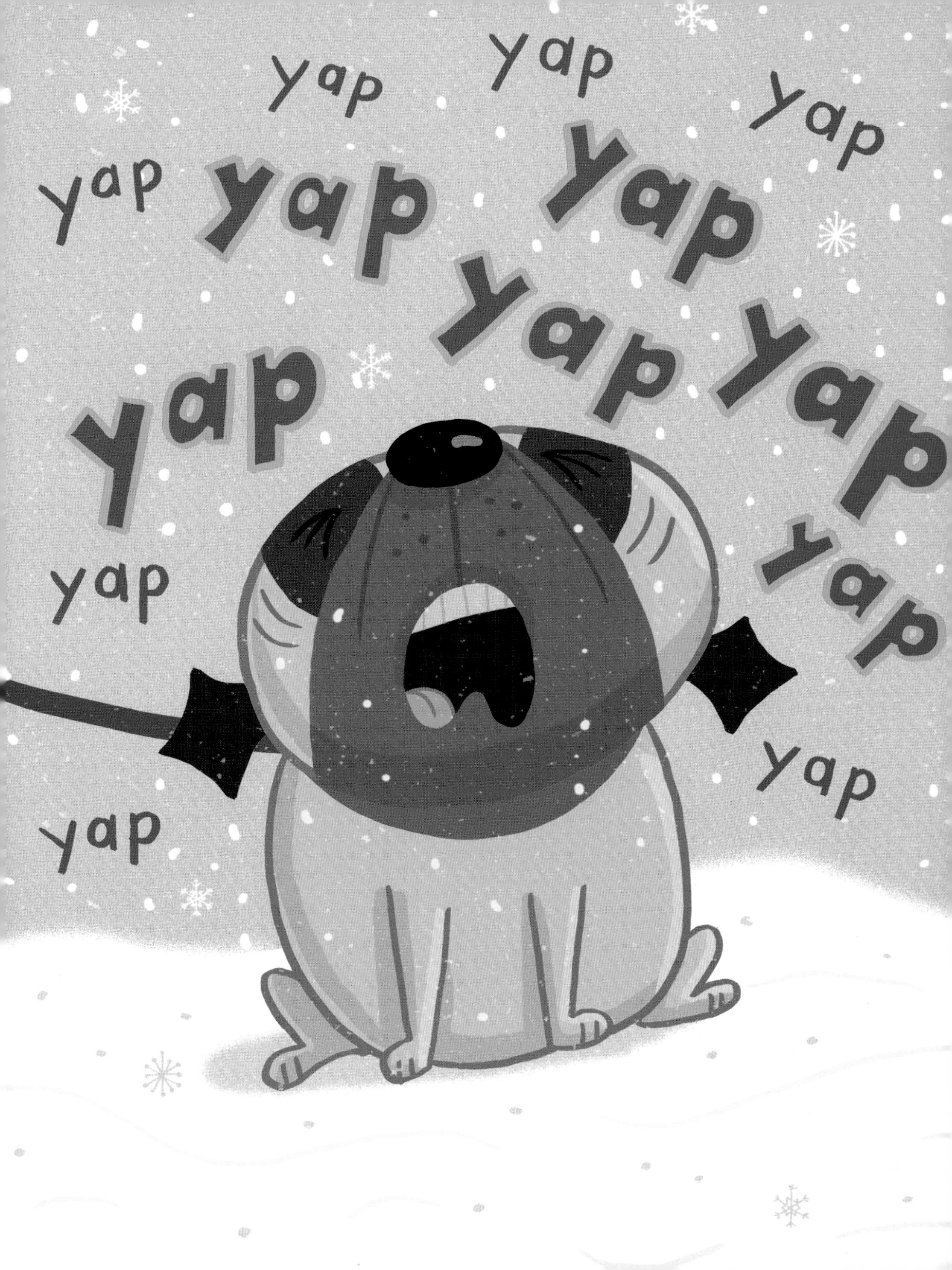
yap
yap
yap
yap
yap
yap
yap
yap
yap
yap
yap
yap
yap

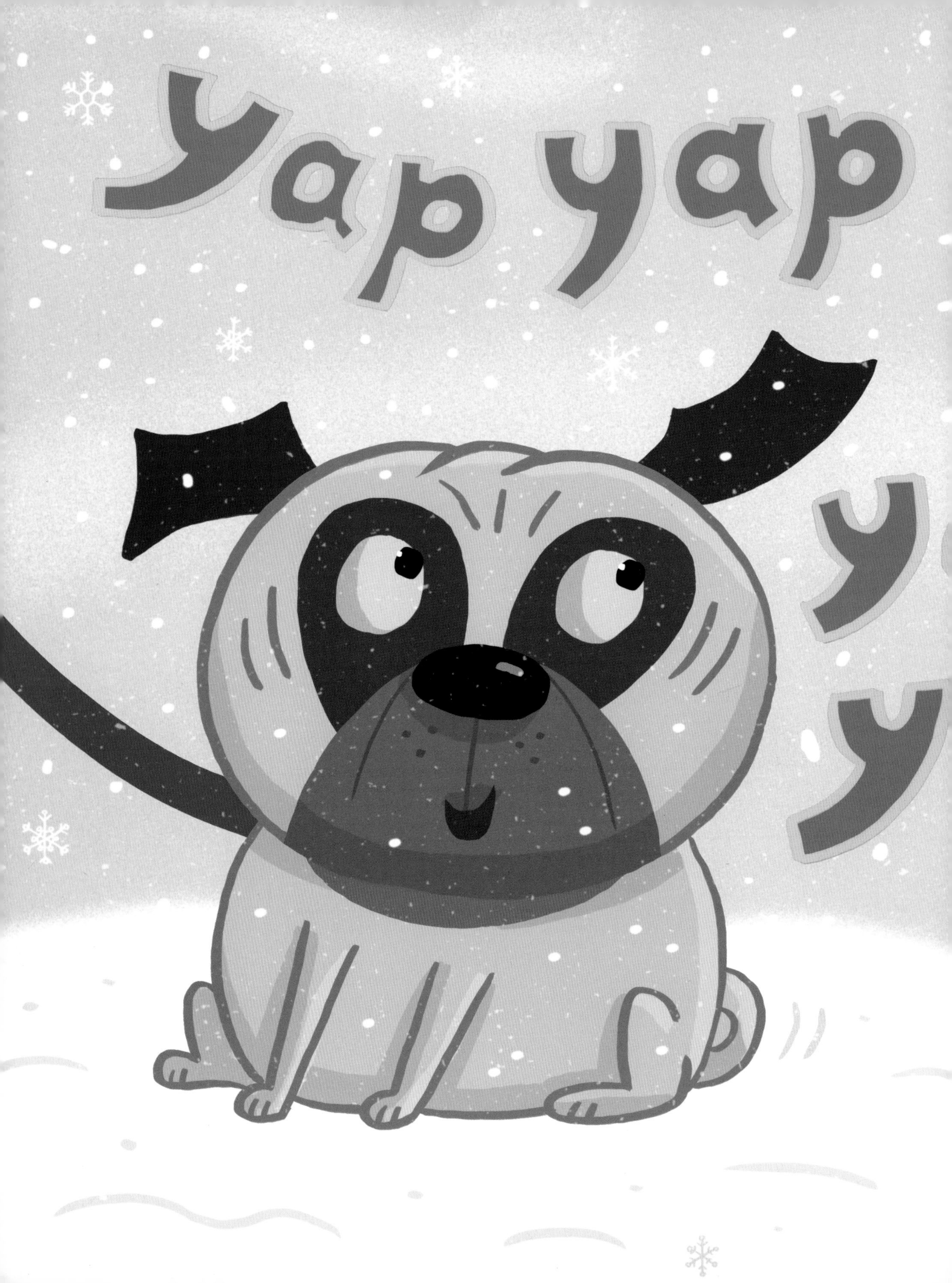
Yap yap

yap yap
yap
yap
yap
yap
yap
yap

Pug sees Peg.

HOLIDAY HOUSE is registered in the U.S. Patent and Trademark Office.
Printed and Bound in April 2016 at Tien Wah Press, Johor Bahru, Johor, Malaysia.
The artwork was created digitally.
www.holidayhouse.com
First Edition
1 3 5 7 9 10 8 6 4 2

Library of Congress Cataloging-in-Publication Data is available.

ISBN 978-0-8234-3645-3 (hardcover)

ISBN 978-0-8234-3688-0 (paperback)

Some More I Like to Read® Books in Paperback

Animals Work by Ted Lewin

Bad Dog by David McPhail

Big Cat by Ethan Long

Can You See Me? by Ted Lewin

Cat Got a Lot by Steve Henry

Drew the Screw by Mattia Cerato

The Fly Flew In by David Catrow

Happy Cat by Steve Henry

Here Is Big Bunny by Steve Henry

I Have a Garden by Bob Barner

I See and See by Ted Lewin

Little Ducks Go by Emily Arnold McCully

Me Too! by Valeri Gorbachev

Mice on Ice by Rebecca Emberley and Ed Emberley

Not Me! by Valeri Gorbachev

Pig Has a Plan by Ethan Long

Pig Is Big on Books by Douglas Florian

Pug by Ethan Long

Up by Joe Cepeda

What Am I? Where Am I? by Ted Lewin

You Can Do It! by Betsy Lewin

Visit http://www.holidayhouse.com/I-Like-to-Read/ for more about I Like to Read® books,
including flash cards, reproducibles and the complete list of titles.